Oregon Trail

Risa Brown

Bethany, Missouri

Photo Credits:
Cover © Photodisc, Library of Congress; Title Page, Page 21 © Photodisc; Page 4 © National Park Service;
Pages 5, 7, 9, 12, 13, 15, 16, 17, 19, 22 © Library of Congress; Page 8 © Eileen Hart;
Page 11 © Rebecca D.M Todd; Page 18 © Coral Coolahan

Cataloging-in-Publication Data

Brown, Risa W.
    Oregon Trail / Risa Brown. — 1st ed.
    p. cm. — (National places)

    Includes bibliographical references and index.
    Summary: Describes life for the pioneer families on the
Oregon Trail, including dangers they faced.
    ISBN-13: 978-1-4242-1370-2 (lib. bdg. : alk. paper)
    ISBN-10: 1-4242-1370-3 (lib. bdg. : alk. paper)
    ISBN-13: 978-1-4242-1460-0 (pbk. : alk. paper)
    ISBN-10: 1-4242-1460-2 (pbk. : alk. paper)

    1. Oregon National Historic Trail—History—Juvenile literature.
2. Overland journeys to the Pacific—Juvenile literature. 3. Frontier and pioneer life—
West (U.S.)—Juvenile literature. 4. Historic roads and trails—Juvenile literature.
[1. Oregon National Historic Trail—History. 2. Overland journeys to the Pacific.
3. Frontier and pioneer life—West (U.S.) 4. Frontier and pioneer life—Oregon.
5. Pioneers—West (U.S.)—History. 6. West (U.S.)—History. 7. Historic roads and trails.]
I. Brown, Risa W. II. Title. III. Series.
    F597.B76 2007
    978'.02—dc22

First edition
© 2007 Fitzgerald Books
802 N. 41st Street, P.O. Box 505
Bethany, MO 64424, U.S.A.
Printed in China
Library of Congress Control Number: 2006940995

Table of Contents

A New Life

In the 1840s, many Americans wanted a better life. The Oregon **frontier** offered a wonderful new life. But getting there was difficult and often dangerous.

The Trail

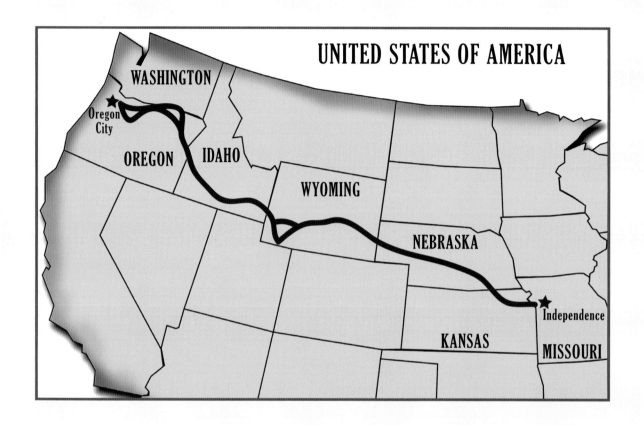

Many traveled on a **route** from Independence, Missouri to Oregon City which was about two thousand miles.

Despite the long trip, people used the
Oregon Trail for more than twenty-five years.

The Wagon

Pioneers used big wagons to carry enough food for six months. They took pots and pans for cooking and tools for farming. There was no room for furniture or many special things.

Animals

Oxen pulled the heavy wagons. Sometimes the pioneers took cows, pigs, and even chickens.

Traveling Together

Families traveled together in **wagon trains**, relying on men who knew the way. As many as a hundred wagons could be in a wagon train so that people could help each other.

A Day on the Trail

People, even children, walked beside the wagons. They woke up before the sun came up and walked until dark.

Making Camp

At day's end, they put the wagons in a circle and had dinner. Sometimes they told stories or would sing, especially if someone brought a fiddle or a **harmonica**.

Dangers

The pioneers faced dangers from harsh weather and wild animals. Disease was the worst danger.

Mountain Lion

Harsh Land

The pioneers crossed rivers that could sweep away wagons and animals. The oxen had trouble pulling the heavy wagons over steep mountains.

New Land

Once in Oregon, the pioneers built farms or started businesses. They made themselves a new life.

Glossary

frontier (fruhn TIHOR) — a land without cities

harmonica (har MON uh kah) — a musical instrument played by blowing on it

oxen (OKS en) — large animals that can pull a lot of weight

pioneers (pye uh NEERZ) — people who are first to settle a new area

route (ROOT or ROUT) — a trail or path used over and over to get from one place to another

wagon trains (WAG uhn TRANES) — a group of people traveling together in large wagons

Index

FURTHER READING

Graham, Amy. *The Oregon Trail and the Daring Journey West by Wagon.*
  Enslow, 2006.
Landau, Elaine. *The Oregon Trail.* Children's Press, 2006.
Quasha, Jennifer. *Covered Wagons: Hands-on Projects About America's Westward
  Expansion.* PowerKids Press, 2003.

WEBSITES TO VISIT

Because Internet links change so often, Fitzgerald Books has developed an online list of websites related to the subject of this book. This site is updated regularly. Please use this link to access the list: www.fitzgeraldbookslinks.com/np/ot

ABOUT THE AUTHOR

Risa Brown was a librarian for twenty years before becoming a full-time writer. Now living in Dallas, she grew up in Midland, Texas, President George W. Bush's hometown.